COMIC CHAPTER BOOKS

SCOOBY-DOO!

STONE ARCH BOOKS
a capstone imprint

Published in 2016 by Stone Arch Books,
A Capstone Imprint
1710 Roe Crest Drive,
North Mankato, Minnesota 56003
www.mycapstone.com

Library of Congress Cataloging-in-Publication Data is
available on the Library of Congress website.

ISBN: 978-1-4965-3583-2 (library binding)
ISBN: 978-1-4965-3587-0 (paperback)
ISBN: 978-1-4965-3591-7 (eBook PDF)

Summary: Scooby-Doo and the Mystery Inc. gang have
tickets to opening night of *Hamlet* at the Crystal Cove
Theater, one of the town's most beautiful buildings. But
Shakespeare's play features only one ghost, not two!
Can Scooby and the gang stop the curse of the stage
fright, or will they get booed out of the theater?

Printed in the United States of America in North Mankato, Minnesota.
009660F16

COMIC CHAPTER BOOKS

SCOOBY-DOO!

written by Steve Korté
illustrated by Scott Neely

CURSE OF THE STAGE FRIGHT

TABLE OF CONTENTS

MEET MYSTERY INC.

SCOOBY-DOO

SKILLS: LOYAL; SUPER SNOUT
BIO: THIS HAPPY-GO-LUCKY HOUND
AVOIDS SCARY SITUATIONS AT ALL
COSTS, BUT HE'LL DO ANYTHING FOR
A SCOOBY SNACK!

SHAGGY ROGERS

SKILLS: LUCKY; HEALTHY APPETITE
BIO: THIS LAID-BACK DUDE WOULD RATHER LOOK FOR GRUB THAN SEARCH FOR CLUES, BUT HE USUALLY FINDS BOTH!

FRED JONES, JR.

SKILLS: ATHLETIC; CHARMING
BIO: THE LEADER AND OLDEST MEMBER OF THE GANG. HE'S A GOOD SPORT — AND GOOD AT THEM, TOO!

DAPHNE BLAKE

SKILLS: BRAINS; BEAUTY
BIO: AS A SIXTEEN-YEAR-OLD FASHION QUEEN, DAPHNE SOLVES HER MYSTERIES IN STYLE.

VELMA DINKLEY

SKILLS: CLEVER; HIGHLY INTELLIGENT
BIO: ALTHOUGH SHE'S THE YOUNGEST MEMBER OF MYSTERY INC., VELMA'S AN OLD PRO AT CATCHING CROOKS.

CHAPTER 1
PLAYTIME

The autumn sun set on Crystal Cove, and the coastal town quickly turned foggy and bone-chillingly cold. Shaggy and his dog Scooby-Doo bounced up and down in the backseat of a brightly colored van called the Mystery Machine. Their pal Fred was driving, and nearby sat Daphne and Velma.

Together, the five of them were known as Mystery Incorporated, a clever gang that solved mysteries around the world.

The gang was on their way downtown to the Crystal Cove Theater for an important evening. Not only was it the opening night of William Shakespeare's *Hamlet*, but there was also going to be a special ceremony before the play. The gang was scheduled to receive an award from the citizens of Crystal Cove for all the mysteries they had solved.

Shaggy and Scooby weren't looking forward to seeing the play, but they were excited for the ceremony. After all, one of their favorite restaurants was catering the event.

"Like, I can already smell those delicious cupcakes. How about you, Scoobs?" Shaggy asked his canine friend.

SNIFF! SNIFF! SNIFF!

Scooby-Doo sniffed at the air. "Ruh-uh!" he agreed. "Rummy!"

"You'll both need to wait a little longer," Velma told them. "Food won't be served until after the play."

"After?!" Shaggy and Scooby exclaimed.

I'M SO EXCITED! THIS PRODUCTION OF *HAMLET* DOESN'T CUT ANY OF THE ORIGINAL TEXT.

IT SHOULD BE A VERY EDUCATIONAL FOUR HOURS!

HAMLET

EDUCATIONAL?

ROUR ROURS?!

DON'T WORRY, GUYS. YOU'RE GOING TO LOVE IT.

HAMLET IS ABOUT A GREAT DANISH PRINCE.

LIKE, DID YOU SAY "DANISH"?

When Shaggy and Scooby heard that word, they smiled and stopped worrying. Unfortunately, neither one actually heard what Velma had said. Shaggy misheard Velma and thought that *Hamlet* was a play about the tasty breakfast rolls known as Danishes.

"Yum!" Shaggy said to his pal Scooby. "Like, maybe we'll be getting some free samples of Danish tonight!"

"Ruh?" Scooby-Doo said, confused. He thought Velma was talking about Great Danes instead of Danishes.

They both turned out to be wrong, of course!

Just then, Fred slammed on the brakes.

SCREEEEEEEEEEEECH!

The Mystery Machine squealed to a stop in front of the Crystal Cove Theater. Giant spotlights outside the theater shined onto the huge Victorian mansion. The mansion had been built many years ago as an opera house, and on this foggy night it glowed like an eerie castle.

"We're here!" Fred told the gang.

"Like, finally," said Shaggy. "Couldn't we have at least stopped for a snack, Fred?"

Fred stepped out of the Mystery Machine, and then opened the van's rear doors to let out the others.

CRAAAAAAAAAASHH!

Dozens of empty boxes of Scooby Snacks spilled onto the ground at his feet.

"I think you two have had enough snacks for one evening," he said.

"Like, those were our pre-snack snacks! Right, Scoobs?" said Shaggy.

Scooby-Doo nodded his head. "Rep!" he barked.

Fred, Daphne, and Velma all sighed. Then they headed toward the theater. Well-dressed citizens of Crystal Cove gathered on the sidewalk.

Outside the entrance, the Mystery Inc. gang stopped to read a giant sign.

TONIGHT
AT THE
**CRYSTAL
COVE
THEATER**
OWNED BY DAVID BELASTIC

HAMLET

STARRING
DAVID BELASTIC

DIRECTED BY
DAVID BELASTIC

PRODUCED BY
DAVID BELASTIC

I GUESS THERE WASN'T ROOM FOR SHAKESPEARE'S NAME ON THE SIGN!

I'M SURPRISED BELASTIC DIDN'T TAKE CREDIT FOR WRITING THE PLAY, TOO!

HOW VERY AMUSING!

YOU MUST BE THAT PESKY GROUP OF KIDS KNOWN AS MYSTERY INC.

"Jeepers!" said Daphne, jumping back. "We didn't see you there."

"A good actor knows how to make an entrance," said the tall, thin man with a sneer. "Yes, it's true. You lucky children are in the presence of the world-famous actor, director, and producer David Belastic. I'll also be playing Hamlet this evening."

As he spoke, Belastic slowly spun in circles to show off his Hamlet costume. The jewel-covered costume sparkled from the top of his velvet cap to the extra-pointy leather shoes on his feet.

Fred leaned over to Daphne, "More like a world-famous ham, if you ask me," he whispered.

Belastic narrowed his eyes at Fred. "What did you just say, young man?" he asked, snarling. "Did you call me a ham?"

"What's so bad about that?" asked Shaggy, confused. "Like, ham is delicious! You can make ham and cheese sandwiches, ham omelettes, ham soup, ham —"

GRUMMMMMMBLE

A loud grumbling sound cut off Shaggy in mid-sentence. Next to him, Scooby-Doo held his hungry stomach.

"Rorry!" said Scooby, apologizing for the interruption.

"That's all right, Scoob! Now where was I," Shaggy continued. "Oh yes, ham casserole, ham and pineapple pizza, ham —"

"Enough!" cried Belastic. There was an angry look in his eyes.

"Sorry about them," interrupted Velma. "They're just excited for tonight's food."

"Well, they're just going to have to wait!" shouted Belastic. "Food won't be served until AFTER the play!"

"Like, we know," said Shaggy, hanging his head in defeat. Scooby-Doo did the same.

Just then, a friendly voice suddenly called out, "You made it! Now we can start the party!"

It was Janet Nettles, the mayor of Crystal Cove. She ran up to the Mystery Inc. gang and gave each member a big hug.

"We are so excited to be giving this award to you," she said with a smile. "The citizens of Crystal Cove really can't thank you enough for your years of —"

Before she could finish her sentence, Belastic interrupted, "Mayor Nettles, I really must protest again. It's bad enough to have a pointless award ceremony for these meddlesome kids on my stage, but what about this flea-bitten dog?" Belastic pointed at Scooby. "You are turning my beautiful theater into a kennel!"

"Rea-ritten rog? Rennel?!" Scooby-Doo exclaimed.

"Like, take it easy, Scoobs," said Shaggy, comforting his pal with a pat on the back. "You haven't had any fleas for months!"

"Reah!" Scooby barked. He could feel himself wanting to itch, but he didn't dare.

Mayor Nettles glared at Belastic. "Perhaps you've forgotten the terms of your agreement with the Crystal Cove city government, Mr. Belastic," she said firmly. "When the city sold this landmarked theater to you, one of the conditions was that you would host civic events, like the one we're having tonight."

"Yes, but —" Belastic began.

"Whether you like it or not!" Mayor Nettles interrupted this time.

Belastic sighed with disgust. Then he wearily raised his hand and pointed the Mystery Inc. gang toward the stage door.

"Let's get this annoying event out of the way," he said and then stomped off.

Shaggy turned to Velma as they walked backstage, "So, like, do we get the pastries before or after the award ceremony?" he asked.

"What pastries?" said Velma, confused.

"Like, you said there'd be Danish pastries!" Shaggy exclaimed.

"Reah, Ranish rastries!" Scooby repeated.

Velma looked at them and shook her head. "Sometimes I don't understand a word you're saying," she admitted.

CHAPTER 2

STAGE FRIGHT

Shortly after, Fred, Daphne, Velma, Shaggy, and Scooby-Doo stood behind the curtain on the stage of the Crystal Cove Theater.

Mayor Janet Nettles stepped up to a podium to introduce them. "Ladies and gentlemen, it is time to honor our very special guests," she said to the sellout audience. "Please welcome Mystery Incorporated. Together, these five individuals have solved countless mysteries in our beloved city!"

CLAP! CLAP! CLAP! CLAP!

The audience cheered.

"It's the most haunted place on Earth!" a voice called out from the audience.

Mayor Nettles forced herself to smile at that comment. "Well, yes," she admitted. "But the Mystery Inc. detectives have also explored supernatural goings-on around the entire world. I'm very proud to honor these brave teens, and Scooby-Doo, of course, with this plaque to show our appreciation."

FWOOOOOOOSH!

The curtain opened, revealing the Mystery Inc. gang. "Hooray!" The audience erupted in cheers.

Fred, Daphne, and Velma stepped forward. They each took a bow. Then they signaled for Shaggy and Scooby to join them.

"Like, after you, Scoobs," said Shaggy.

"Rhy rhank rou!" Scooby-Doo replied, stepping forward.

Unfortunately, Shaggy was stepping on Scooby-Doo's paw. The clumsy hound staggered forward, did a triple somersault, and landed in a split on the front of the stage.

"ROWWWW!" Scooby howled in pain.

The audience groaned.

"Are you all right, Scoobs?" Shaggy asked his fallen friend.

Scooby-Doo slowly stood. When he did, the crowd erupted in wild applause. They thought that the whole thing had been planned.

After a moment, Mayor Nettles began, "Before we start this evening's production of *Hamlet*, does anyone in the audience have a question for our guests of honor?"

A loud, high-pitched voice called out from the back of the audience, "Yes, yes, I have a very important question for the detectives!"

The gang watched a woman dressed all in black and wearing large sunglasses march up the aisle and stand in front of the stage.

MY NAME IS MS. ELLIE WILSON.

I AM THE WORLD'S MOST SUCCESSFUL GHOST-HUNTER.

RUH-ROH!

ZOINKS!

MY QUESTION FOR THEM IS WHETHER THEY ARE WORRIED ABOUT THE GHOST THAT HAUNTS THE CRYSTAL COVE THEATER!

NO MORE QUESTIONS!

THIS FOOLISHNESS IS TAKING TIME AWAY FROM MY PLAY!

David Belastic shooed Mayor Nettles and the Mystery Inc. gang offstage and then motioned to the lighting man in the back of the theater. As the theater lights began to dim in the auditorium, the gang moved to their seats in the audience.

"That's odd," said Fred. "I've never heard any stories about a ghost in this theater."

"Me neither," said Daphne. "Maybe we should have a talk with Ms. Wilson after the play."

Velma guided Scooby-Doo and Shaggy to seats in the middle of a row. "I don't want the two of you sneaking out before the play is over," she said. "Get ready for four hours of high culture!"

"Zoinks!" Shaggy exclaimed.

"Roinks!" agreed Scooby.

Suddenly, the curtain went up and bright lights shined onto the stage. The stage now looked like the top of a large castle, and two actors marched back and forth across the set.

"Who's there?" asked one of them.

"Nay, answer me: stand and unfold yourself," said the other.

"Like, 'Unfold yourself'? What does that mean? What language is this?" Shaggy whispered to Velma. "Sounds boring to me."

"Yeah," Scooby-Doo agreed. "Roring!"

"Shhh," Velma whispered back. "It's Elizabethan English, of course. Shakespeare wrote this play in the 1600s."

It was going to be a very long four hours!

Shaggy sunk back into his seat. He closed his eyes. *If I can't be eating food,* he thought. *At least I can be dreaming about it!*

Scooby-Doo had the same idea.

* * *

Five minutes later, more actors had arrived onstage, including one who was playing the ghost of Hamlet's dead father. Velma glanced over at Shaggy and Scooby-Doo.

Both were already sound asleep!

"Wake up!" she said, elbowing Scooby-Doo. "You're going to miss the ghost!"

"Rhost?!" Scooby exclaimed. He jumped up in his chair and grabbed Shaggy.

"Relax, Scoobs," Shaggy said, calming his pal. "It's just some actor wearing a sheet. Like, I've seen better ghost costumes on Halloween!"

Then one of the actors onstage started shouting and pointing. "Look, there it comes again!" he said. The ghost in the sheet flapped its arms and tried to look scary.

Suddenly, a second ghost appeared onstage. This ghost glowed with a sickly green color. **WHOOOOOOOOOOOOOOO!** It moaned.

Shaggy and Scooby squinted their eyes for a better look.

"Like, check out those special effects, Scoobs!" Shaggy exclaimed. "How did they make that ghost look see-through?"

"Roah!" Scooby exclaimed, perking up in his seat.

POOF!

With a burst of sulfurous smoke, the ghost disappeared from view.

"Eeeek!" Audience members screamed and jumped up from their seats. They fled from the theater in a panic.

A man accidentally stepped on Daphne's foot and pushed his way past her. "Ouch!" she cried, but the man didn't look back.

"Like, we're out of here! Right, Scoobs?" Shaggy asked his pal.

"Ruh-huh!" Scooby-Doo agreed.

"Hang on, gang!" shouted Fred. "The five of us aren't going anywhere. It looks like we have a mystery to solve!" With that, he and Daphne ran to the front of the theater and climbed up on the stage.

"Like, I was afraid he was going to say that!" Shaggy gulped. "How about if Scoobs and I stand guard outside the theater? No sense in all five of us making this ghost angry."

Velma reached into her pocket and pulled out two boxes of tasty treats. She shook the boxes and smiled at Shaggy and Scooby.

"Wouldn't you guys rather stay here and enjoy a tasty Scooby Snack?" she said sweetly.

"Like, where'd you get that?" Shaggy asked. "I thought we ate them all!"

"Reah," Scooby agreed, surprised.

Velma ripped open the brand-new boxes. The smell of Scooby and Shaggy's favorite treats filled the theater. The two friends hungrily licked their lips.

"I never leave home without an emergency snack stash for you guys," Velma told them.

"Well, okay," Shaggy said, thinking about his options. "We might stay if you make it two each!"

"Deal!" said Velma.

Scooby-Doo and Shaggy approached Velma. They each snagged a box from her hands.

YOINK!

"Hey!" Velma cried.

Scooby-Doo and Shaggy weren't listening. They each lifted a box over their mouth and tipped it upside down. Dozens of Scooby Snacks fell from the boxes, into their mouths, and directly down their throats.

GULP! GULP! GULP!

"That sure hits the spot! Right, Scoob?" said Shaggy, searching the box for crumbs.

"Ruh-huh!" Scooby agreed. "Rummy!"

"You said two each!" Velma protested.

"Like, we know," Shaggy exclaimed. "Two boxes each. I guess you still owe us one!"

"HA! HA!" Fred and Daphne couldn't help but laugh.

"They got you there," said Daphne.

Shaggy winked at Scooby-Doo and whispered to his pal, "It works every time!"

As Velma walked to the front of the theater to join her fellow detectives, she thought to herself, *It works every time!*

She didn't care that they'd eaten them all. Velma only cared that they were now going to help the gang crack the case!

CHAPTER 3
BACKSTAGE BATTLES

Fred quickly gathered the Mystery Inc. detectives onstage. "Okay, gang," he said, "let's put our heads together and see if we can figure this mystery out."

KLUNK! Shaggy and Scooby-Doo knocked their heads together as they both reached for a Scooby Snack that had fallen to the floor.

"Like, ouch!" said Shaggy, rubbing his forehead. "I don't think that's what Fred meant when he told us to put our heads together, Scoobs!"

"Rouch!" agreed Scooby.

Velma sighed and then looked around. "Where did that ghost expert Ellie Wilson go?" she wondered aloud. "I think I'll see if I can talk to her. She might be able to shed some light on this mystery."

"That's a great idea, Velma," said Daphne. "Fred and I will go backstage and see what we can find."

Just then, David Belastic stormed onto the stage. The actor was still dressed in his Hamlet costume, and his pointy boots echoed on the hardwood floor of the stage. He was not in a good mood.

"What are you troublemaking kids up to now? My play is ruined, and my theater is haunted!" he yelled. "Worst of all, Crystal Cove will never get to see my groundbreaking performance as Hamlet!"

Scooby and Shaggy giggled at that last comment, which earned them a fierce glare from Belastic.

"Didn't you hear what the ghost said?" demanded Belastic. "Anyone who remains in this theater is doomed."

"Like, does that mean the dinner is cancelled too?!" Shaggy asked, afraid of the answer.

"Of course it does!" cried Belastic.

"But what about all the food?" Shaggy said.

"The food? What does it matter?" shouted Belastic, growing annoyed. "They can throw it in the trash, for all I care!"

"Rhe rash!" Scooby cried out.

"Zoinks!" exclaimed Shaggy at the thought.

"Who cares about the food? What about me?" the actor continued. "I will have no choice but to tear down my beautiful theater. I will be ruined! My brilliant acting career is over!"

"Mr. Belastic," said Fred. "We want to help you solve the mystery of this theater ghost!"

Belastic snarled at the teens. "If I wanted your help, I would ask for it! If you don't leave, I'll have you arrested for trespassing!"

With that, Belastic marched offstage and slammed the door of his office.

WHAM!

"Time for Mystery Inc. to grab this ghost!" said Fred. "Let's split up and meet back here in fifteen minutes. We have to work fast before Belastic comes through on his promise."

Fred and Daphne each ran backstage.

Shaggy turned to Velma. "Um, Velma," he started, "don't you think that Scoobs and I should take some Scooby Snacks with us?"

"Sorry, guys," she said as she walked to the front of the theater. "You already ate my emergency stash and my emergency emergency stash. I'm all out!"

"Darn," said Shaggy.

"Rarn," agreed Scooby.

Then Shaggy had an idea. "I might know where we can find some food!" he told his friend, who followed closely behind him.

* * *

Daphne wandered over to the other side of the stage.

CREEEEEAK! She slowly pushed open a door with rusty hinges.

WHAM!

The door slammed behind Daphne, startling her. When her eyes adjusted to the dark, she discovered that she was in a room full of dusty stage props. There was a rusty suit of armor, a table piled high with swords and other medieval weapons, and a statue of an angry-looking black raven.

BLAM!

Daphne jumped again when she heard a sudden noise from the other side of the theater. That was the direction where Fred had gone.

What was that noise? she wondered. Then she called out, "Fred! Are you okay?"

"I'm fine," he yelled back. "Keep searching for clues."

Daphne sighed with relief. Now she just had to look for clues in this creepy room. She walked over to the suit of armor and slowly lifted the visor on the helmet, not sure what she was going to find. Fortunately, the suit was empty.

She carefully handled the prop weapons. There was no clue about the ghost there.

Then she put her hand on the raven statue. "I wonder what play this raven prop was used in," she said as she tilted the statue toward her.

Suddenly, a secret trapdoor opened right beneath her.

WHOOOSH!

"Jeepers!" cried Daphne as she plummeted through the open door.

A split-second later, she landed on the floor of a tiny pitch-black room. *THUD!*

"Ouch!" Daphne cried.

Luckily, she wasn't hurt, and she quickly switched on her flashlight to see where she had landed.

The room was dirty and covered in rotting wood. Looking up, she saw the trapdoor above her, but it was too high for her to reach.

Then she heard a sound.

DRIP!

DRIP!

DRIP!

DRIP!

"That sounds like a leaky faucet," Daphne said to herself.

She looked up and saw water trickling down from the trapdoor above.

"Hello?" she called out. "Who's there?"

No one answered.

Just then, the flow of the water increased.

WHOOOOOOOSH!

The puddles around Daphne's feet grew larger. Soon, she was standing in several inches of water. The room was filling with water, and she was trapped!

JEEPERS! THIS ISN'T GOOD!

I CAN'T REACH THAT DOOR!

NOW'S THE TIME TO USE MY YOGA TRAINING AND SEE HOW LONG I CAN HOLD MY BREATH!

I'LL WAIT UNTIL THE WATER IS ALMOST TO THE TOP OF THIS ROOM. READY . . . ONE . . . TWO . . .

PHEW!

Daphne was soaking wet but unharmed. Next to the trapdoor she saw the thick fire hose that had filled her room with water, but there was no sign of a ghost or anyone else. She turned off the water and wondered what had happened.

Did someone try to drown me? she thought. *Was it the ghost?*

With an angry shake of her wet hair, she marched out of the room determined to solve the mystery.

* * *

Meanwhile, Shaggy and Scooby-Doo searched the backstage area of the theater. Shaggy peeked his head into one doorway and then the next, growing more and more frustrated as they went along.

"Like, it has to be around here somewhere, Scoobs!" Shaggy said.

"Rhat?" Scooby-Doo asked, confused.

"The kitchen, of course!" Shaggy replied.

Shaggy looked inside another doorway. Nothing. He wasn't giving up. All the other guests had fled the Crystal Cove theater. That meant a whole lot of leftovers, and Shaggy couldn't wait to try them — after all, he'd never had leftovers before!

"Rhis ray!" Scooby-Doo said, pointing down a long, narrow hallway.

"How do you know that?" Shaggy asked.

Scooby-Doo lifted his long snout into the air. **SNIFF! SNIFF! SNIFF!** He gave a sniff and then licked his lips.

"Good work, Scoobs! Lead the way!" Shaggy instructed.

SNIFF! SNIFF! SNIFF!

Scooby-Doo sniffed his way down the hall with Shaggy following closely behind. As they neared the end of the hallway, a strange sound echoed through the building.

WHOOOOOOOOOOOOOOO! It moaned.

"Like, what was that?" Shaggy asked.

Scooby-Doo lifted his nose from the floor. "Ra R-r-r-rhost?!" he suggested.

"Like, m-m-maybe it was just the w-w-wind," Shaggy offered. He grabbed onto Scooby-Doo, and they both shivered in fright.

Suddenly, the hallway lights flickered out. Shaggy and Scooby-Doo couldn't see anything in the pitch-black darkness — luckily, they were still hanging onto each other.

WHOOOOOOOOOOOOOOO! The ghoulish moan came again.

Just then, a ghostly figure appeared at the other end of the hallway. It glowed a sickening green, just as it had on the theater stage.

"Zoinks!" Shaggy shouted.

"Roinks!" Scooby repeated.

"Hear my warning!" the ghost said again. "This theater is cursed and must be destroyed. Anyone who stays here will be sorry!"

"Like, we're already sorry!" Shaggy said, still clinging to Scooby-Doo.

"Reah!" Scooby agreed. "Re're rorry!"

"Too late!" cried the ghost.

WHOOOOOOOOOOOOOOOO!

The green ghost floated toward them. Shaggy and Scooby had to leave — and fast! Shaggy felt his way down the darkened hallway, pulling Scooby behind him by the collar.

"In here!" Shaggy said as they ducked inside the nearest room.

SLAM!

They quickly closed the door and locked it behind them.

WHAM!
WHAM!
WHAM!

Scooby-Doo and Shaggy held each other as something beat on the door. After a few minutes, they couldn't hear the ghost anymore. They figured they were safe.

"Phew!" said Shaggy. "That was close!"

SNIFF! SNIFF! SNIFF!

Shaggy could hear Scooby-Doo sniffing at the air. "What is it, boy? Do you smell something?" he asked.

"Reah," Scooby confirmed. "Rood!"

"Food?!" Shaggy exclaimed. "We must be in the kitchen! I wish we could see." Shaggy tried the light switch, but it didn't work. "Oh well. You'll just have to point me in the right direction, Scoobs."

SNIFF! SNIFF! SNIFF!

Scooby-Doo sniffed at the air again. He could smell strawberries and coconut and vanilla and cucumbers and bubble gum!

"Rover rere!" he barked, pulling Shaggy toward the mouth-watering aroma.

SNIFF! SNIFF! SNIFF!

Scooby-Doo felt around a long table, which was covered with dozens of sweet-smelling items. "Roah! Rancy!" he said, picking up one that smelled extra sweet.

"Like, I believe the French call these hors d'oeuvres," said Shaggy, grabbing a handful for himself. "Dig in!"

CHOMP! CHOMP! CHOMP!

Shaggy and Scooby-Doo quickly ate as much of the feast as they could. Nearly everything on the table was gone before they even stopped to chew.

"Um, Scoobs?" said Shaggy, hesitantly. "Does this food taste a little funny to you?"

"Res, runny!" Scooby agreed.

Suddenly, the lights flickered back on. Scooby-Doo and Shaggy each saw a stranger standing in front of them.

"G-g-g-ghost!!" Shaggy screamed.

"R-r-r-rhost!!" echoed Scooby.

The two friends ran in opposite directions. They tripped and stumbled over chairs and tables and fell to the floor with two loud **THUDS!**

"Rouch!" Scooby-Doo moaned in pain.

"Scoobs? Is that you?" Shaggy asked from the other side of the room.

Scooby-Doo lifted his head off the floor. His face was covered in white powder, and a ring of redness surrounded his lips. He looked like a canine clown.

"Zoinks!" Shaggy shouted.

"Roinks!" Scooby repeated when he spotted Shaggy. His face looked the same way!

"What happened?" Shaggy wondered. He looked around at the room, puzzled. Then he opened the door. On the door was a sign that read *Makeup Room.*

"Like, this isn't the kitchen, Scoobs," he told his friend.

"Ruh?" Scooby-Doo asked.

"It's a makeup room!" Shaggy replied. "And that wasn't food. It was —"

"Rakeup?!" finished Scooby.

"Exactly! Makeup!" said Shaggy as he frantically spit and wiped his face.

"Yuck! Patooey!" Scooby-Doo spit.

The two stood in awkward silence. Then Scooby finally picked up a cherry-flavored lipstick, shrugged, and bit off half of it.

After a moment, Shaggy said, "Pass me that blackberry eye shadow, will you, Scoob?"

CHAPTER 4
FOOD FIGHT

KNOCK! KNOCK!

"Mr. Belastic, are you in here?"

KNOCK! KNOCK!

Velma knocked on the door of David Belastic's office a second time, but there was still no answer.

She slowly opened the door and peeked inside. There was no sign of Belastic, but there was a large wooden desk in the middle of the room, piled high with papers.

Behind the desk stood an ornate throne, covered in jewels and painted gold.

"Jinkies, look at that throne!" said Velma. "Maybe Belastic really does think he's the Prince of Denmark."

Velma had been unable to find Miss Ellie Wilson, so she decided to do some detective work and explore the rooms in the theater. The first stop was David Belastic's office. Velma quickly browsed through the papers on Belastic's desk. Then she brought out her high-tech smartphone.

"Let's see what I can find out on the Internet," she said as she activated her phone and settled down on Belastic's golden throne.

Ten minutes later, after she had studied more than a dozen websites — **BZZZZT!** — her phone buzzed with the sound of an incoming text.

The screen read, "Unknown number."

"That's odd," said Velma. "I wonder who is sending me a text."

Before she could read the text, the door to Belastic's office slammed shut.

CRASH!

Velma ran to the door and pulled on the handle. It was locked from the outside. Someone — or something — did not want her to leave the office!

BZZZZZT!

Velma looked down at the text on her smartphone.

"I warned you to leave the theater," it read. "Now let's see if you are afraid of the dark!"

Velma laughed when she read the message. "I haven't been afraid of the dark since I was two years old, Mr. Ghost," she called out confidently. "You're going to have to do better than that to scare me!"

WHOOOOOSH!

Velma looked up and noticed a thick black fog creeping into the room. It was pouring out of a heating vent near the ceiling.

The fan on Velma's phone blew all the fog out of the room. With a smile, she then removed a bobby pin from her pocket and inserted it into the lock of the door. She jiggled the pin for about a minute.

CLICK!

Velma unlocked the door. Then she turned the knob, exited the office, and went to find her friends.

"I wonder where Scooby and Shaggy have disappeared to," she said.

* * *

As it turned out, Scooby-Doo and Shaggy had wandered into a dark and remote part of the theater, far away from the stage. They were now completely lost.

"Like, I told you we should've turned right back there," Shaggy told his pal.

"Ro," Scooby argued. "Reft!"

Shaggy and Scooby both sighed. It was dark, they were lost, and — most importantly — they were hungry! The pair slowly felt their way along a narrow, pitch-black passageway.

Shaggy accidentally stepped on Scooby-Doo's tail again.

"Rouch!" Scooby-Doo howled. He jumped in pain and knocked over Shaggy. The two of them tumbled down a short flight of stairs and crashed through a door.

CRAAAAASH!

"Like, ouch is right!" agreed Shaggy as he felt for bruises after their tumble down the stairs.

The duo had landed inside a small room, and it took a minute for their eyes to adjust to the brightly lit surroundings. In one corner of the room stood a giant mirror. Next to that was a cabinet loaded with jars and tubes of stage makeup.

There was a sign on the door that read David Belastic.

It was Belastic's dressing room!

Then Shaggy and Scooby saw something that made them forget about their aches and pains.

On a wooden table in the middle of the room sat a platter of a dozen cupcakes! Shaggy nearly fainted with happiness. Actually, he did.

WHAM!

Shaggy hit the floor — hard. He lifted his head and shook it, like he was awakening from a dream. But this wasn't a dream!

"Like, are you seeing what I'm seeing, Scoobs?" Shaggy exclaimed.

But Scooby couldn't answer. He was gobbling up a cherry cupcake as fast as he could.

CHOMP! CHOMP! CHOMP! CHOMP!

"Move over, Scoobs!" said Shaggy as he joined his pal at the cupcake platter and grabbed a vanilla cream cupcake.

Just then, a chilling voice filled the room.

"I hope you enjoy those treats," it said. "Because it's the last meal you will ever eat!"

It was the glowing ghost hovering nearby!

ZOINKS! THE GHOST!

I'LL TEACH YOU TO IGNORE MY WARNING!

I HAVE AN IDEA, SCOOBS.

TAKE THAT, MR. GHOST!

GULP!

DID YOU REALLY THINK YOU COULD STOP ME . . . WITH A CUPCAKE?

WHOOOOOOOOOOOOOOOO! The ghost moaned.

WHOOOOOOOOOOOOOOOO! It moaned — even louder and angrier than before.

"It was good knowing you, Scoob!" Shaggy told his canine friend.

"Rou roo!" said Scooby.

Then they both closed their eyes and hoped for the best.

Just when it appeared that the ghost was going to grab Shaggy, the door to the dressing room slammed open.

CRASH!

Fred, Daphne, and Velma burst into the room. As soon as they arrived, the ghost disappeared in a cloud of smoke.

POOF!

After the smoke faded away, Fred crouched down and brought out his magnifying glass. While he studied the floor of the dressing room, Scooby walked over to Velma and Daphne.

SLURP!

Scooby-Doo gave each of them a big, sloppy kiss, soaking them with slobber.

"Um, thanks, Scooby," said Daphne.

"Scooby and I sure are glad to see you guys," said Shaggy. "Like, how did you find us?"

"When I was looking through the papers on Belastic's desk, I saw a delivery note about a dozen cupcakes to be delivered to his dressing room," explained Velma. "I knew that any place with cupcakes was the most likely place to find you!"

Shaggy flushed. "Like, this was definitely the first place we looked," he said. "And we certainly only ate real food today. Right, Scoob?"

CHOMP! CHOMP! CHOMP! CHOMP!

Scooby wiped frosting from his mouth. "Reah," he agreed. "Ro rakeup!"

"What did he say?" asked Daphne.

"Never mind," said Shaggy, embarrassed.

IT SOUNDED LIKE HE SAID "MAKEUP."

NOPE. WE DIDN'T EAT ANY MAKEUP TODAY, DID WE, SCOOBS?

UM, SCOOBS?

SCOOBS! SAVE SOME FOR ME!

NO TIME FOR CUPCAKES, GANG. WE STILL HAVE A MYSTERY TO SOLVE, AND VELMA HAS A PLAN!

LIKE, ARE YOU SURE THE PLAN DOESN'T INVOLVE EATING JUST ONE MORE CUPCAKE?

YES, I'M SURE!

CHAPTER 5
GHOST-CATCHERS

"So, like, what's the big plan?" Shaggy asked as the gang worked their way through the dark hallways of the theater. "Is it time to call the Crystal Cove police?"

"No police," said Fred. "We need to solve this mystery ourselves."

"Fred's right, you two," said Velma. "We came here to receive an award for solving mysteries. What would it look like if we just gave up on this one and went home?"

"It would look pretty good, if you ask me!" said Shaggy with a smile. "Like, there aren't any ghosts at home."

Scooby-Doo nodded beside him.

"What about the cupcakes?" Velma shot back. "There aren't any cupcakes at home either!"

"We don't want those to go to waste, do we, Scoob?" Shaggy added nervously.

"Rope!" declared Scooby-Doo.

"Then finish this case with us, and you can have all the cupcakes you want," said Velma.

"Ripee!" shouted Scooby-Doo.

"Velma's right. But for now, the cupcakes will have to wait," said Daphne. "We're going back to the stage where the ghost first appeared."

Shaggy and Scooby exchanged nervous glances. Both of them thought that the best plan would be to jump into the Mystery Machine and put as many miles as possible between them and the Crystal Cove Theater!

Scooby-Doo and Shaggy each shoved as many cupcakes as they could into their mouths.

CHOMP!

CHOMP!

CHOMP!

CHOMP!

Then they reluctantly followed their fellow teammates.

* * *

Ten minutes later, the Mystery Incorporated detectives gathered on the Crystal Cove Theater's main stage.

"So here's the plan," explained Velma. "We are going to stand on this stage and try to get the ghost to reappear."

"Rat's razy!" declared Scooby.

"Like, I gotta agree with my buddy Scoobs," added Shaggy. "That is totally crazy!"

"Crazy or not, it's our best chance to solve this mystery," declared Fred. "So let's get started!"

SO, MR. GHOST, YOU WERE LOOKING A LITTLE GREEN EARLIER.

WAS IT SOMETHING YOU ATE?

DO YOU WANT TO PLAY A GAME WITH US?

HOW ABOUT HIDE-AND-GHOST-SEEK?

DO YOU KNOW HOW TO INTRODUCE YOURSELF TO A GHOST? YOU SAY, "HOW DO YOU BOO?"

"HOW DO YOU BOO?" THAT'S A GOOD ONE, FRED!

RUH-HUH!

YOU MEDDLESOME KIDS JUST MADE YOUR LAST JOKE!

ZOINKS!

WATCH OUT FOR THAT NEXT STEP. IT'S A KILLER!

OKAY, DAPHNE. GRAB THE ROPE!

GOT IT!

LIKE, WHAT'S HAPPENING?!

WHOOOOOOOOOOOOOOOO!

Shaggy and Scooby-Doo watched with amazement as Fred and Daphne jumped through the ghost and ran offstage!

"Scoobs, they're running away!" Shaggy cried out as he covered his eyes. "We're doomed!"

"Roomed!" agreed Scooby as he put a giant paw in front of his eyes.

"Goodbye, old friend," Shaggy told him.

"Roodbye!" Scooby said with a sob.

"Like, haven't we already said this today, Scooby?" asked Shaggy.

"Rep!" said Scooby-Doo.

Like before, Shaggy and Scooby nervously opened their eyes. The ghost was gone! There was just a trail of drifting smoke in front of them.

"We did it, Scoobs!" yelled Shaggy. "We scared the ghost into disappearing! We —"

ARRRRGH!

Before Shaggy could finish his sentence, there was a strangled cry of anger offstage.

"Let me go! This is an outrage! Just wait until I call the police," yelled David Belastic as Daphne and Fred pulled the angry actor onstage.

Belastic was tightly tied up in the rope.

Velma stepped forward and said with a smile, "No need to call the police, Mr. Belastic. I just took care of that. And they are going to have lots of questions for you!"

"Gang, I'd like you to meet the ghost of the Crystal Cove Theater — Mr. David Belastic himself!" Fred exclaimed.

"What?! This is an outrage! How did you meddling kids . . . when did you know?" sputtered Belastic.

"The first clue was the footprints that your pointy-toed Hamlet boots left on the floor every place that the ghost appeared," said Fred.

"And Velma did some sleuthing online," Fred told them.

"That's right," Velma continued. "First, I discovered that Miss Ellie Wilson, the so-called 'ghost expert,' is really your wife. And searching through the Crystal Cove real estate records, I learned that years ago you tried to have this same theater condemned so that it would be torn down."

"Rorn down?" asked Scooby-Doo.

"Like, wouldn't that make it hard for him to be a hammy actor?" Shaggy suggested.

"Yes, it probably would have ended his acting career," Velma agreed, "but Belastic knew that the theater is sitting on top of a huge untapped reservoir of oil deposits. If he had been able to have the theater destroyed, he could have made a fortune selling the rights to drill for oil."

Fred held up a tiny projector so that everyone could see it. "I found this in his pocket," he explained.

Fred passed the projector around. "It's a miniature infrared ray projector," he continued. "Belastic hid from view and used this machine to project the glowing green ghost, hoping to scare everyone away from the theater so that he could close it."

Fred lifted his other hand high in the air.

"High fives, everyone!" he called out. "The Mystery Inc. detectives have solved another mystery!"

SMACK!
SMACK!
SMACK!

Three hands came together.

"Wait, where are Shaggy and Scooby?" asked Daphne.

Velma sighed. "Two guesses."

Meanwhile, back in David Belastic's dressing room, Shaggy and Scooby-Doo congratulated themselves on solving the mystery of the Crystal Cove Theater ghost.

And what better way to celebrate than to personally take charge of the Crystal Cove Theater cupcake disappearance!

CHOMP! CHOMP! CHOMP! CHOMP!

BIOGRAPHIES

STEVE KORTÉ is a freelance writer. At DC Comics he edited more than 500 books. Among the titles he edited are *75 Years of DC Comics*, winner of the 2011 Eisner Award, and *Jack Cole and Plastic Man*, winner of the 2002 Harvey Award. He lives in New York City with his own super-cat Duke.

SCOTT NEELY has been a professional illustrator and designer for many years. Since 1999, he's been an official Scooby-Doo and Cartoon Network artist, working on such licensed properties as *Dexter's Laboratory*, *Johnny Bravo*, *Courage the Cowardly Dog*, *Powerpuff Girls*, and more. He has also worked on *Pokémon*, *Mickey Mouse Clubhouse*, *My Friends Tigger & Pooh*, *Handy Manny*, *Strawberry Shortcake*, *Bratz*, and many other popular characters. He lives in a suburb of Philadelphia.

COMIC TERMS

caption (KAP-shuhn)—words that appear in a box; captions are often used to set the scene

gutter (GUHT-er)—the space between panels or pages

motion lines (MOH-shuhn LINES)—illustrator-created marks that help show movement in art

panel (PAN-uhl)—a single drawing that has borders around it; each panel is a separate scene on a spread

SFX (ESS-EFF-EKS)—short for sound effects; sound effects are words used to show sounds that occur in the art of a comic

splash (SPLASH)—a large illustration that often covers a full page or more

spread (SPRED)—two side-by-side pages in a comic book

word balloon (WURD BUH-loon)—a speech indicator that includes a character's dialogue or thoughts; a word balloon's tail leads to the speaking character's mouth

GLOSSARY

condemned (kuhn-demd)—stated that something is unsafe

meddlesome (MED-uhl-suhm)—interfering with the activities and concerns of other people in an unwanted or unwelcome way

medieval (mee-DEE-vuhl)—to do with the Middle Ages, the period of history between approximately A.D. 500 and 1450

podium (POH-dee-uhm)—a raised platform for a speaker, performer, or the leader of an orchestra

reservoir (REZ-ur-vwar)—a natural or artificial holding area for storing a large amount of water

sulfurous (SUHL-fur-uhs)—of, relating to, or containing sulfur, a yellow chemical element found in gunpowder and matches

Victorian (VIK-tor-ee-uhn)—relating to or typical of the period from 1837–1901 when Queen Victoria ruled England

VISUAL QUESTIONS

1. Illustrators draw motion lines to help show movement in art. In this panel (page 63), what do the arcing lines beside Shaggy's head tell you about his action? Can you find other motion lines in this book's comic panels?

2. The way a character's eyes and mouth look, also known as their facial expression, can tell you a lot about how he or she is feeling. In this panel (page 24), how do you think Scooby and Shaggy are feeling? Use the illustration to explain.

3. Pages 68–69 use comic book art to tell the story. How could that part of the story be told using only words? Write one page of text describing what is happening in those illustrations.

4. Sound effects, called SFX for short, are a great way to make a comic book panel come to life. List all the sound effects in this book to make your own SFX dictionary!

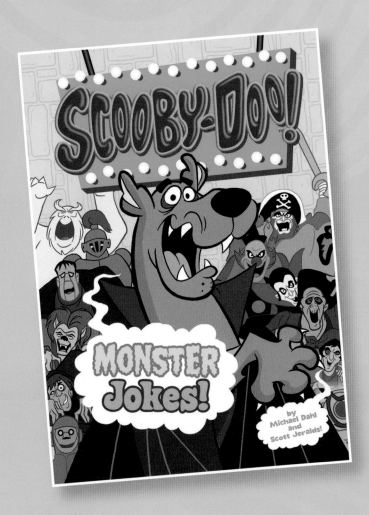

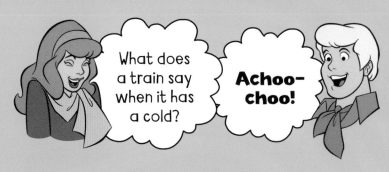

What does a train say when it has a cold?

Achoo-choo!

Why can't the train play music?
It's on the wrong track.

Did you hear about the fire at the circus?
The heat was in tents!

Did you know that ghost has a girlfriend?

Yes, but I don't know what she sees in him!

How do fleas travel from place to place?

THEY ITCH-HIKE!

Why did the vampire flunk out of art class?
She could only *draw blood!*

What do you call a nervous witch?
A twitch!

What's Frankenstein's favorite dessert?
I scream!!!

FIND MORE SCOOBY-DOO JOKES IN...

ALSO FROM CAPSTONE.

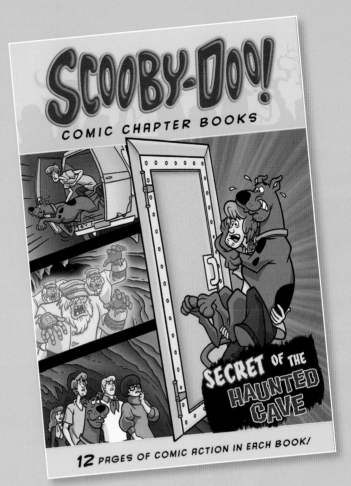

SCOOBY-DOO!
COMIC CHAPTER BOOKS

SECRET OF THE HAUNTED CAVE

12 PAGES OF COMIC ACTION IN EACH BOOK!

SCOOBY-DOO!
COMIC CHAPTER BOOKS

LEGEND OF THE GATOR MAN

12 PAGES OF COMIC ACTION IN EACH BOOK!

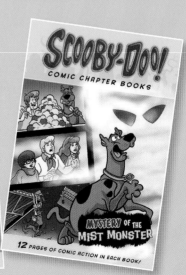

SCOOBY-DOO!
COMIC CHAPTER BOOKS

MYSTERY OF THE MIST MONSTER

12 PAGES OF COMIC ACTION IN EACH BOOK!

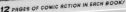

Discover more at

WWW.CAPSTONEKIDS.COM

Find cool websites and more
books like this one at

WWW.FACTHOUND.COM

Just type in the
BOOK ID: *9781496535832*
and you're ready to go!